The Berenstain Bears
GO OUT FOR THE TEAM

CHAMP

When little bears first
Show a will to compete,
It's hard for parents not to
Jump in with both feet.

A FIRST TIME BOOK®

The Berenstain Bears
GO OUT

Stan & Jan Berenstain

Random House 🏠 New York

FOR THE TEAM

Library of Congress Cataloging-in-Publication Data
Berenstain, Stan. The Berenstain bears go out for the team. (A First time book)
Summary: Brother and Sister Bear are such good baseball players
that Papa Bear decides they should try for the Bear Country Cub League.
ISBN 978-0-394-87338-1 (trade) — ISBN 978-0-375-98255-2 (ebook)
[1. Baseball—Fiction. 2. Bears—Fiction.] I. Berenstain, Jan. II. Title.
III. Series: Berenstain, Stan. First time book.
PZ7.B4483Beok 1986 [E] 85-30164
Printed in the United States of America   74 73 72 71 70 69 68 67 66 65 64 63 62 61

Brother and Sister Bear, who lived with their mama and papa in the big tree house down a sunny dirt road deep in Bear Country, enjoyed the changing seasons—and the sports that went with them:

—football and soccer in the fall . . .

—basketball and
ice hockey in the
winter . . .

—and their favorite,
baseball in the spring.

As soon as Brother and Sister felt the first warmth of the spring sun, they got out their trusty ball, bat, and gloves and began limbering up for the season.

They played pitch-and-catch . . .

and practiced batting.

Why, they even studied up on the rules of the game.

Pretty soon some of their friends came to join in the baseball fun.

After a while Brother looked around and said, "Hey, I think we have enough for a game. Let's go over to Farmer Ben's back meadow and choose up sides."

Farmer Ben was a good neighbor. He had been allowing cubs to play baseball in his meadow for years. Of course, the grassy meadow wasn't a real baseball field, so there were a few problems and some special ground rules.

There were no foul lines, just base paths worn by year after year of cubs running the bases. So there were a lot of arguments about foul balls. There was a rule against sliding into second base, because second base was a rock. And any ball that was hit into the duck pond in left field was a ground-rule double and an automatic time-out while they fished it out.

But arguments, rocks, and duck ponds
didn't worry Brother, Sister, and
their friends. They chose up sides
and started a game.

Sister had done some growing since last season, and when she went to bat she whacked her very first ground-rule double. All the cubs—and even the ducks—were surprised.

And her knowledge of the rules came in handy when Cousin Freddie forgot to touch second base on his way to third. She called for the ball, tagged second, and declared him out. He made a big fuss, but she pointed out that those were the rules.

"Isn't that right?" she asked Farmer Ben, who was watching from the sideline.

"Right as rain," said Farmer Ben.

The game moved right along until
Brother hit a ball all the way into
the next field and Farmer Ben's
goat got it.

"Back so soon?" asked Papa, looking up from his paper as Brother and Sister trooped back home.

"Yep!" said Sister, holding up the ball. "Game called off on account of Farmer Ben's goat chewing the cover off the ball."

Papa was pretty impressed when he heard about Brother's hit and Sister's ground-rule double.

"Seems to me," said Papa, "that you cubs might want to think about playing some real baseball on a real baseball field. It says right here in the paper that the Bear Country Cub League is going to be holding tryouts pretty soon. You might want to sign up."

"Now, hold on," interrupted Mama. "That's a high-powered league over there, and those tryouts involve quite a lot of pressure."

"Pressure?" asked Sister. "What do you mean?"

"You'll be competing against lots of other cubs and not everybody is going to make the team," said Mama. "But you both play pretty well," she added, "so it's up to you."

"Won't hurt to drive over and have a look," said Papa.

"Wow!" said Brother when he saw the Cub League field. It was a real field with fences and foul lines and real bases and grandstands and everything.

And the teams wore uniforms! Brother and Sister signed up right then and there!

BEAR COUNTRY CUB LEAGUE

LAST YEAR'S CHAMPS.

SIGN UP HERE

They got ready for the tryouts by practicing. They practiced fielding and hitting. Mama showed them how to choke up on the bat against fast pitching. They even practiced bunting and base running. But as tryout day drew near, they began to get a little nervous.

"Try to calm down," said Mama. "It's only a game. Besides, the worst that can happen is that you won't make the team. You can always try out again next year."

"No, that's not the worst that can happen," said Brother, looking gloomy. "The worst that can happen is if Sis makes the team and *I don't*!"

"I consider that a sexist remark!" snapped Sister angrily.

"Well, not completely," said Mama. "After all, Brother's older than you and he's very proud of his baseball ability."

"I see what you mean about pressure," said Sister.

Finally the day of the tryouts came. There were cubs all over the field—and league officials with clipboards and sunglasses so you couldn't see what they were thinking. Each cub had a number, and the officials moved around the field watching the cubs and making checks on their clipboards. Talk about pressure!

Brother and Sister were nervous at first. Sister missed an easy ground ball and Brother swung too hard at bat, missed the ball completely, and fell down on the seat of his pants. But as the tryouts continued, they both settled down and did a little better.

Brother remembered to choke up on the bat. He hit a good single and went to second base when the fielder bobbled the ball. Sister fielded some grounders well, and once when she was batting, the catcher dropped the third strike and she ran to first base even though she had struck out. There was a big fuss, but an official was watching and said she was right.

"Well, how did you do?" asked Mama when she and Papa came to pick the cubs up after the tryouts.

"Hard to say," answered Brother. "We certainly weren't the best."

"But we weren't the worst, either," said Sister. "Anyway—it's only a game and the worst that can happen is that we won't make the team."

"Yeah," sighed Brother. "We can always try again next year if we want to."

"When will you know?" asked Papa as they headed home.

"They're going to post the results on the bulletin board tomorrow," said Brother.

"Well," said Papa the next day, "don't you think we ought to drive over and check up?"
"I guess so," said Brother.
"May as well," said Sister.

When they reached the field, Brother and Sister ran to the bulletin board.

"Talk about pressure," said
Papa, mopping his brow as he
and Mama waited in the car.
"Indeed," said Mama, fanning
herself.

At last Mama and Papa heard a shout as Brother and Sister burst out of the crowd around the bulletin board.

"We made it! We made it!" they shouted, jumping for joy.

"There are four teams in the league!" shouted Sister. "The Cardinals, the Bluejays, the Orioles, and the Catbirds! We both made the Cardinals!"

"Terrific!" said Papa.

"Congratulations!" said Mama.

On the day of the first game, the cubs looked elegant in their uniforms, and Mama and Papa sat up front in the grandstand. Brother was up to bat against the Bluejays. The pitcher wound up and threw a fast ball. Brother watched it go by.

"Strike one!" called the umpire.

"That was no strike!" screamed Mama, waving her hat. "It was wide by a mile! Call yourself an umpire!"

"Mama, please!" hissed Sister from the sideline. "Calm down! And remember— it's only a game!"

"Sorry about that," said Mama. Then
she straightened her hat, sat down, and
enjoyed the rest of the game.